My Universe

A collection of poems & short stories

Rusiru Tharana Kodithuwakku

Published by Rusiru Tharana Kodithuwakku

A catalogue record for this book is available from the British Library.

ISBN 978-0-9931725-0-2

First Published in 2015 in Great Britain.

Cover design & page setting by Jeevendra Bandara Ranasinghe.
Printed in Sri Lanka by Vijitha Creations Pvt Ltd.

My Universe

A collection of poems & short stories

Rusiru Tharana Kodithuwakku

Illustrated by: Rusiru Tharana Kodithuwakku

This book is dedicated to...

* My mother, who passed on her wonderful talent of writing to me and supports me throughout my life,
* My father who teaches me all the hard things about life,
* My grandmother for passing her poetry skills down the generation & for being a second mother to me,
* And of course my little brother, Seniru, for being the best brother in the world!

"'My Universe' is a glimpse of my interpretation of the infinite universe written in the language of Literature..."

Acknowledgements

I would wish to make a special note of gratitude for all my Teachers so far. The Staff of Noah's Ark Nursery, Aberdare, Mrs Bethel (the Headteacher of Roberts' Town pre-school) & Staff, Mrs Faith Williams, Mrs Stephanie Draper, Mrs Lisa Parry, Mrs Sarah Furnival, Mrs Diane Davies, Mrs Natalie Drew and Mr. Dave Allen (Teachers of Abernant Primary School), Miss Rhian Davies, Mrs Janet Meyrick, Mrs Claire Davies, Mrs Paula Loring, and Mrs Susan Jones (Assistant Teachers of Abernant Primary School), Mr Mike Hawkins (Ex-Headteacher of Abernant Primary School), Mrs Caryl Hamer (Deputy Headteacher of Abernant Primary School) and Mrs Julie Kucia (the Headteacher of Abernant Primary School)for making my Primary School days very happy, memorable and treasured.

I would also like to give heartiest thanks to my uncle, Dr. Priyal Perera for the photography, Jeevendra Bandara Ranasinghe for making the cover design & pages a reality, Vijitha Creations Pvt Ltd and Jayanath Kalubowila (in Sri Lanka) for taking care of all the workload of the printing.

At last but not least, my Mother and Father for making my dream of publishing a book at 11 years of age come true.

Rusiru Tharana Kodithuwakku
Abernant, Aberdare, UK.
December 2014
sarasimadara@yahoo.com

Foreword

"Children who read for pleasure and fun open up new worlds. They embark on journeys. They step into other people's shoes and walk around in them." (Organisation for the Economic Cooperation and Development, 2000).

The statement above epitomises Rusiru's enthusiasm and commitment to reading and writing. His work in this book demonstrates his ability to use his experiences and knowledge of texts to create worlds that take other people on journeys. He uses language to create vivid images and to bring characters and events alive. As his Headteacher I am extremely proud of Rusiru and loved reading his many pieces. In particular his narrative, "The mouse who travelled through time." In this piece there is much evidence of his effective use of language.

"One night he had a brainwave. He was devouring a meal of the finest cheese with Rat when all of a sudden his expression went wild with exhilaration as he seized a blackboard and chalk stick, then began to skim over the board leaving an elaborate sketch of a Time Machine, an unimaginably perfect Time Machine but it was surprisingly fuelled by mouldy cheese."

Another example comes from his letter to Willy Wonka.

"When I found out that I had the final Golden Ticket, I felt as though I could reach the universe with my fingers, yes, I was that proud. Outside the colossal, towering gates, I could literally taste the airy chocolate with the tip of my tongue. Before very long the gates opened and we went inside the intricate building accompanied by the one and only Mr. Willy Wonka himself."

The Organisation for the Economic Cooperation and Development also state that:

"A reading child is a successful child."

As you will see from this work Rusiru is a child who reads, is a child who is successful and is a child who I'm sure will be very successful in all his future endeavours.

Mrs. Julie Kucia
Headteacher
Abernant Primary School

Foreword

When given the honour of being asked to write a foreword for Rusiru's collection of writings I felt compelled to quote the following.

"I have always imagined that paradise will be a kind of library."

- Jorge Luis Borges -

"The more that you read, the more things you will know. The more you learn, the more places you'll go."

- Dr. Seuss -

Through his writings Rusiru has always demonstrated a love of literature in all its forms. His enthusiasm and commitment to writing and his use of language to transport us to new worlds is both inspiring and exciting. As one of his primary teachers both in his infant and early junior years I feel an enormous pride in Rusiru and so enjoyed reading this collection, in particular the poem 'That Flowing River' which demonstrates his effective use of figurative language:

At last the river calms, flowing in slow strides
Collecting with it magnificent tides
The proud river gushes gracefully
As it comes to rest in the continual sea.

I also loved reading his narrative 'The Plants, the Professor and the Mystery' where he uses language so vividly to build tension and hold the attention of the reader:

"Me neither," said John, brushing away cobwebs from his hair. "Come on." They walked on and finally met their destination: the cobwebbed streets of Shadow Lane. They searched for the right door and knocked. There was a few seconds of silence and then the thud of footsteps was heard and the door slowly opened revealing a person with wispy grey hair and a wrinkled face. "Well, well, well, what do we have here, eh?" he rasped.

Neil Gaiman states that "Books make great gifts because they have whole worlds inside of them."

I am confident that Rusiru will have great success in his world and will open many new worlds for others through his literary skills and I wish him love and luck for the future.

Mrs. Sarah Furnival

Class Teacher- Year 2 & 3

Foreword

Rusiru is a talented young man who has a natural creative flair when it comes to writing. His collection of work highlights his love of literacy. This is a delightful analogy of stories and poems written by Rusiru. An author in the making of which I have no doubt.

Mrs. Diane Davies

(Class teacher-Year 4)

Foreword

These examples of literacy work are a snapshot of Rusiru Kodithwakku's extensive ability. In addition to a creative mind he has the skills in place to learn and develop into an outstanding student. What impresses me the most is his ability to achieve through all areas of literacy, producing work of an exceptional standard.

I have had the opportunity to teach Rusiru and pleasure of reading his work first hand. He is the most thoughtful, well-mannered and able student I have taught. Rusiru is a genuinely hardworking, mature and talented pupil who I have no doubt will go on to fully attain his potential.

Good Luck Rusiru!

Mr. Dave Allen

Class Teacher (Year 5 & 6)

Contents

The Universe

The universe is everlasting
Sometimes it is flabbergasting
To the past you can travel,
Mysteries you might unravel,
Sometimes things are curiously magic,
Sometimes things are very tragic,
In time when we come to the brim
Big Bang Two might begin...

The Solar System

Mercury has a lot of cliffs,
While Venus's clouds are very stiff,
Earth has a job of supporting life,
When Mars's surface is as rusty as a knife,
The asteroid belt is between Mars and Jupiter,
It is filled up with planetary litter
Jupiter has a lot of mass,
And Saturn's rings are really class,
Uranus is as cold as a tyre,
Neptune is nowhere near fire,
Pluto is definitely not in sight,
And say thank you to the sun for giving us light.

My shoes took control of me

My shoes took control of me,
They even took me to school,
So when it made me dance,
It made me like a fool,

They started to ignite,
Then took me into space,
They took me past many stars,
I was flying, this was ace,

I landed on a planet,
Which was home to an alien,
I gave it my shoes,
It spoke like an Australian,

I headed back but crash landed in NASA,
They were searching for aliens by picking up clues,
"What did you do?" screamed an Astro biologist,
I replied "I just found an alien thanks to my shoes."

The Boy Who Liked Football

RING! RING! RING! The bell went, representing the start of break. Abruptly, with the sound of a thousand Saturn V rockets igniting, all the children from Class 6A sprinted down the hallway and into the playground. In the dust roused up by the children, there was a silhouette of a skinny person wearing glasses and clutching a pile of ancient books. This was Isaac Perera. He was an extremely skinny little fellow with steel-rimmed glasses which magnified his tiny eyes. He had a like for football; he would go to the park on weekends and practice kicking a ball but, and here comes the big but, he was useless at it. No matter how much he trained he was useless.

Today, Isaac had brought is his own football and took it out onto the yard proudly. He ambled nervously onto the yard wondering whether the other boys would like his champions league ball and approve of it...

“Hello, Robert,” greeted Isaac, Robert was the top dog in Isaac’s school and he was also a bully. “Do you want to play a game of football with my ball?”

"Your ball, why would we want to play with your ball?" scoffed Robert,

"Erm, well, seeing you don't have a ball I thought you could play with mine,"

"Huh, as if, we'd rather have no ball than have your ball," smirked Robert and then added, "It's probably as useless for football as you are,"

That was the limit; Isaac had had enough of Robert treating him like an animal. Isaac would practice and practice so much that he would be exceptional at it and show Robert that anyone can play football!

After dinner, Isaac cycled to the park with his ball in his backpack. When he got there he started practicing dribbling and skills and then shooting and passing. However, there wasn't any sign that Isaac was getting better so he sat down and thought.

"The football try-outs are on tomorrow and the best players would be able to represent their school so I've got to improve now, but how?" thought Isaac, and then it clicked "Science!" Now, Isaac Perera was exceedingly good at science and maths and now set about finding some paper and a pencil. Then he drew some complex equations and intricate diagrams...

The next day, as Isaac walked to the try-outs he met Robert with his cronies (Robert being the top dog that he was, had cronies – big, well-fed looking boys who would follow him everywhere and anywhere. The only instance where Robert would be seen alone is when he needed to go to the toilet). "What on Earth, you even dared to come to the try-outs, hah, you won't get in; certainly not." said Robert and with a malicious look on his face he strolled off looking smug.

When it was Isaac's turn to shoot Robert shouted "Ha, ha, look at the skinny shrimp!" This distracted Isaac and his shot rocketed away from the goals, and when it was Isaac's turn to pass, one of Robert's cronies gave a fake sneeze and again Isaac failed.

Unfortunately, the coach announced that Isaac hadn't made it.

He went home thinking that he would go to the tournament anyway.

A week later, Isaac and his dad were at the tournament and they watched as Isaac's school pass the first round and the second and the third and the fourth. Then they got into the finals and lost two men because of injury and another for a red card. And then with no substitutes left, another player got injured and then, totally unexpected the coach came up to Isaac and whispered "You have to go out there and play, we're 1-0 down and we need to win. Here, chuck this on," and the coach handed him a pair of shorts, a top, shin pads and boots. Isaac, without thinking, put on the kit and walked out onto the pitch. As soon as Isaac's boots touched the flattened grass a ripple of chatter sounded from the crowd and then Robert's father shouted to the coach "What are you doing? That boy can't play football, are you out of your mind?"

"You know what – I might be!" replied the coach "Just watch the match..." Meanwhile, Robert had the ball and was steaming up the pitch and at the same time Isaac was sprinting up the wing and asked for the ball "No way!" Robert answered and for the tiny fraction of a second taken to look at Isaac, Robert got tackled. The ball soared through the air and was on a trajectory aimed for Isaac, in that split-second calculations whizzed through Isaac's mind like gunfire and worked out the velocity, acceleration and mass of the ball and then almost instantly Isaac's leg whipped the ball in a perfect side volley which sent the ball whistling through the air and into the back of the net. Suddenly, a magnificent round of applause sounded from the spectators and Isaac stood still savouring the moment...

THE END

Ten Things Found in Buzz Aldrin's Spacesuit

A specimen of lunar rocks,
And a spare pair of smelly socks.
A teddy for cuddling whilst in terror,
And a felt tip pen for an unexpected error.
A Hasselblad camera for taking pictures,
And a rusty toolbox for making fixtures.
A sharp razor for shaving,
The US flag for waving.
A card saying congratulations,
And a copy of the Magnificent Desolation.

I Visited the Planet Mars

I visited Planet Mars,
I'll give you information,
About the time when,
I got globally famous,
I was flying to Mars,
Seeing clusters of stars,
I landed on the ground,
I had made it safe and sound,
Then I saw it, a mechanical display,
In which the colour of all were steel grey,
Then I had the exquisite idea of making a museum,
I thought I'd make it a bit like the Aberdare Coliseum,
The museum contained all the probes sent to Mars for every-one to see,
I think my name went down the path of history.

The Mystery of the Stolen Park

Chapter 1

The school bell rang representing the end of school and Ralph Sunstone rushed out of the classroom carrying his heavy books and bumped into the Headmaster "Watch where you're going Sunstone!" Exclaimed Mr Waspsting "Sorry sir, I couldn't see where I was going," replied Ralph and without another word he ran home.

The next day, in school Mrs Honeycomb made an announcement: "We are going to have a new mini park; it is going to have swings, roundabouts and slides." The children cheered "Yay!"

And that was the start of a mystical mystery!

Chapter 2

After school had finished Ralph ran down the field of the budding flowers and through the rusty ancient gate into the pristine park which glowed with cheerfulness. The children and his best friend were there as well. His best friend was Jeremy Thinstring because he was as thin as a string. He was playing on the swings "Shall I push you Jeremy?" Ralph asked "Yes, please Ralph," replied Jeremy.

***

After school Ralph visited the park again...But this time there was a surprise awaiting him! In the space

where there was supposed to be the slides was a monstrous hole!

Chapter 3

Ralph went investigating but all he found were some tiny footprints. He deducted that they were made by some kind of animal.

At home Ralph asked his dad “Which kinds of animals dig holes and have very tiny feet?”

“Well, I can only think of two animals and those are the rabbits and moles but you can’t expect to see them because they’re shy in a way and stay in their burrows.

***

The following day, Ralph had finished his work and was hurrying for his next lesson which was biology.

In general, Ralph thought biology was tedious but today was another story. Mr. Grindstone was the biology teacher and took care of the school allotment and even bred some animals.

When Mr. Grindstone was droning on about exotic plants and herbs, Ralph interrupted and asked "Have you bred moles and rabbits?"

"Why, I have, quite near the school actually," replied Mr. Grindstone and Ralph could tell that the conversation was over.

Chapter 4

Ralph decided to catch the thief red handed so in the middle of the night Ralph asked Dad if he could go outside and rushed into the innovative park now as dark as a blackboard. He hid behind a thicket of bushes and waited, it seemed like endless hours all combined together and then suddenly he glimpsed a shadow stirring, Ralph fixated his eyes on the shadow and searched for lengthy ears but saw none. "Aha," Ralph thought "It's not a rabbit, therefore, it must be a mole!" Then it began digging around the roundabout, rapidly the hole casually got deeper and then longer and vice versa. Eventually, the hole got big enough to let the roundabout slide down and Ralph heard the soft thud of the roundabout hitting the sodden earth. He ran to the hole and looked downwards, what he saw was astonishing, little moles were actually playing in the slides and now the roundabout.

Chapter 5

Ralph went home and the following day, Ralph told Mr. Waspsting and very generously he made a duplicate of everything just for the little moles.

THE END

Football

Football, football
is a game, Much adored,
it has a lot of fame, Football,
football is renown, For many of
its players and their goals, Football,
football, for their teams the fans all
cheer, For losing is their very worst
fear, Football, football, the striker
shoots, BANG!!! The keeper saves it
with a flick of his boot, Football,
football, pass it around, there's
no time to fret, All you have
to do is kick the ball in
the net.

Dinosaurs

Some dinosaurs are as big as Titanic
Some eat food that is organic
T - Rex is scary,
But Troodon is wary,
Pterosaurs fly looking for prey,
When herbivores down below cry in dismay,
Velociraptors are cunning,
But Compsognathus is good at running,
Though these I mentioned
Who today are in extinction
Have talents, they weren't enough mature
To see what was coming due to nature
And so we humans rule for evermore
Far, far in time from the last dinosaur.

The Discovery of Jamie Jameson

Chapter 1 -

Now as we all know there has been outstanding scientists including, Albert Einstein, Isaac Newton, Louis Pasteur, Thomas Alva Edison and Stephen Hawking, but there wasn't a discovery more exciting than the discovery I'm just about to tell you and all this happened in the 2050s, when fridges, television, computers were a bit old – fashioned, in that time they had everything except the fact that some of them were voice-activated! So now let's get to the story.

In the city of London in a large area lived Jamie Jameson. He was only nine years old but he was very intelligent, he lived with his mum and dad in a good quality house with a huge garden so then he could play in it. Even though he was nine, Jamie worked in a science lab with other great scientists.

One day, when he was working in the lab, he suddenly cried out "Eureka, Eureka, I've got it!" one of the assistants asked what the matter was. Jamie replied "I've worked out the way how to time travel!"

"Then you must tell it to someone," said the assistant. "No I'm not going to do that, I'm going to do something else but I can't tell you," said Jamie hurriedly and without speaking to anyone, he went to the Restricted Section of the lab, as he first entered the room he saw his own creation; The Remarkable Rocket.

- Chapter 2 -

Jamie mounted The Remarkable Rocket, he set all that needed to be set and started the countdown,

5, 4, 3, 2, 1, BLAST OFF and The Remarkable Rocket was launched into space. As he was flying in space he saw all kinds of things such as, colossal galaxies, scorching stars and unknown planets but he wasn't looking for that, he was searching for black holes and white holes.

Now Jamie was 600,000,000 km away from the Earth and he wanted something to eat so he switched the gravity activator and the auto pilot on, then he got some sandwiches and a bottle of water.

After he had finished he kept on looking for the black hole and the white hole. He checked on his black and white hole radar and it said that there was a black hole right beside The Remarkable Rocket, and too right it was. It was titanic and looked dangerous, and then suddenly he felt a lurch and another and another, The Remarkable Rocket almost did a back flip, it was the black hole, Jamie pressed the turbo boost and it was like a tug of war, Jamie fired the engines full blast and eventually managed to get out of the black hole's grasp.

-Chapter 3-

After Jamie had gone 100 metres away from the black hole he turned on his white hole attractor and waited, after what felt like hours he saw a white hole emerging from the pitch black dimness!

" I have to make them clash together," thought Jamie and then he had an idea "If I go behind the black hole, the white hole will follow the attractor and it will collide with the black hole," Jamie concluded and his plan worked! Not only did the two get bigger but changed colour too, they turned into a pearl-grey wormhole!

-Chapter 4-

"I've been looking forward to this moment for years and the time has eventually come," he thought and plunged The Remarkable Rocket into the wormhole and suddenly he was at Earth. "How peculiar, I'm back at Earth, well at least it looks like Earth," he thought but just then he heard a spine-chilling, blood-curdling 'R-O-O-O-A-A-R!"

It was a dinosaur! Jamie had actually travelled into the past. He studied some plants and algae and took some photos. He was wandering about when suddenly he laid his eyes on a family of Triceratops trotting out of some dense trees and following him. Wherever Jamie went the triceratops did too, and that's when a brilliant idea clicked in this elaborate brain of his...

-Chapter 5-

Jamie activated the auto-pilot and took a snooze while he travelled back to the hazy blue marble, Earth.

****

By the next morning, everyone was crowded around a tall transparent metal fence in the national history room. The situation was chaotic: people had mobiles glued to their ears and their mouths were moving so fast they were blurred and spit was spraying everywhere, professors were putting forward their theories and arguing and some were just mesmerised, their mouths hanging motionless. But amid all of the commotion, in the metal fence you could see a family of Triceratops in flesh and blood, sleeping serenely.

Jamie Jameson just smiled.

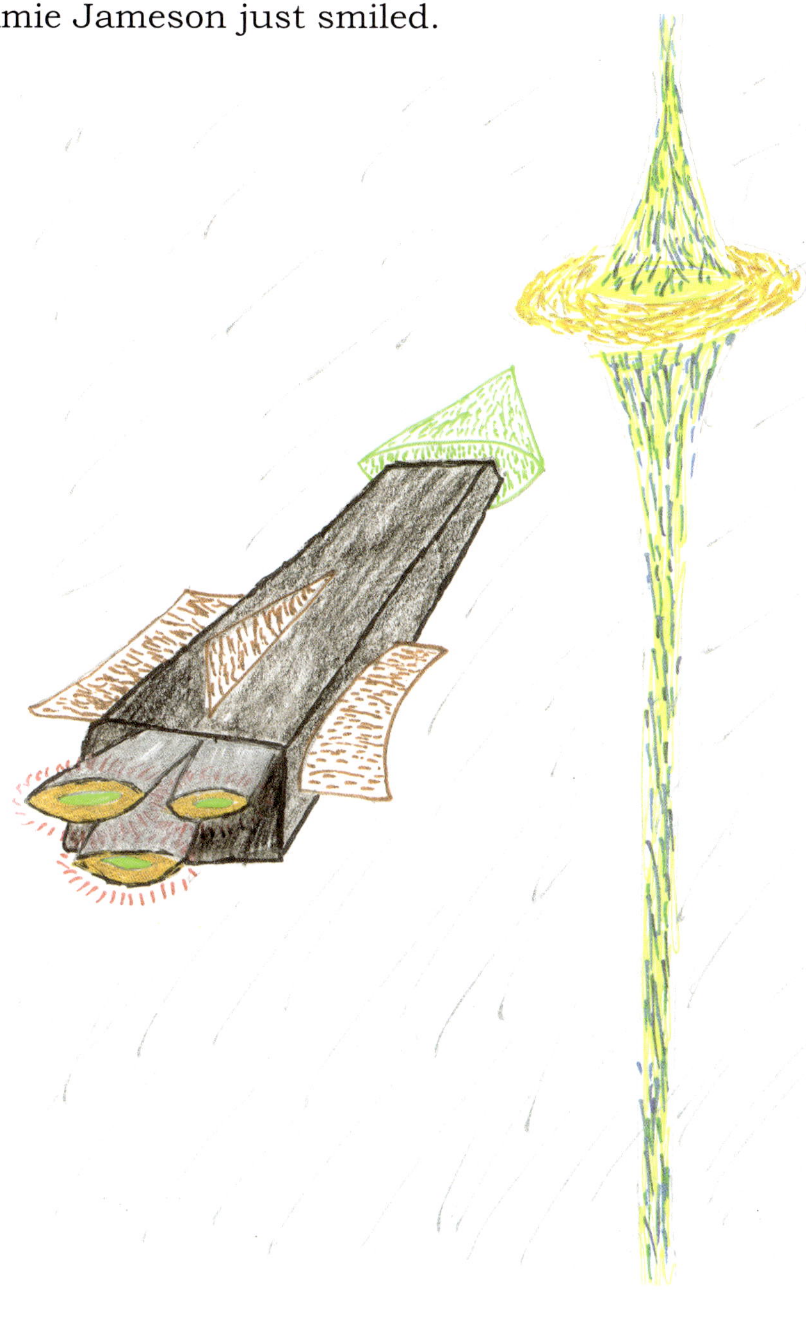

I am a snake in captivity

I live in the busy, boring, dangerous city,
People goggle at me when they go past,
Saying "Oh, look at that snake isn't it vast,"
The zoo-keepers only give me a dead mouse to eat,
Even though I deserve rather finer meat,
Why would they do this to a cobra this fine?
If they replaced me in the jungle the pleasure would be mine,
I know that I was a talented thief,
But as they say anyone can turn over a nice, new leaf.

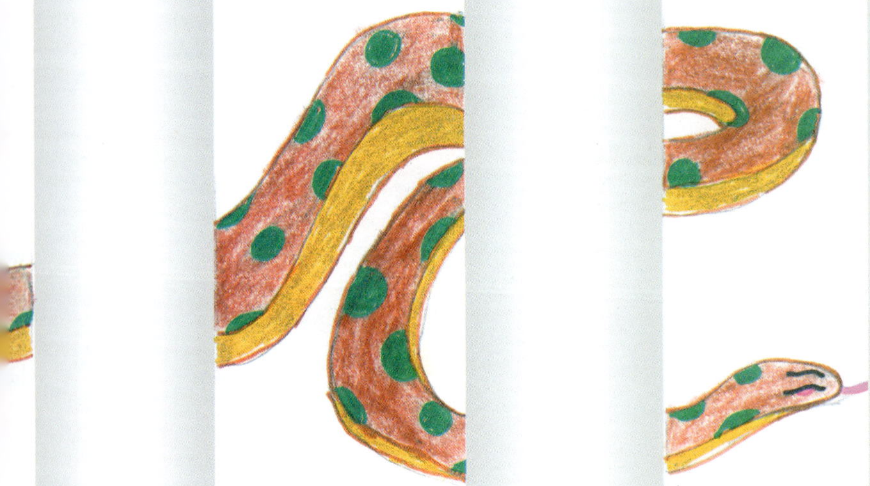

THE ALPHABET

A is for apples that grow on trees,
B is for very, busy bees,
C is for cats whom doesn't like mice,
D is for the dots that are printed on dice,
E is for a fun expedition,
F is for fun that you have loads on a mission,
G is for goat that climbs up mountains,
H is for H_2O that make up fountains
I is for igloo where Eskimos live,
J is for jelly which is not to put in a sieve,
K is for kites that are usually bright,
L is for lions which prowl at night,
M is for mile that you measure length,
N is for newt which has a little strength,
O is for orange which has an amount of acid,
P is for porcupine that's very, very placid,
Q is for queen, who is very royal,
R is for rake which combs up soil,
S is for snake that coils when things are frightening,
T is for thunder that goes well with lightning,
U is for umbrellas that protect us from heat and rain,
V is for violin that can sometimes cause pain.
W is for water, elegant with each drop,
X is for X-rays, where you can see your ribs in the top,
Y is for yellow-eyed penguins, whose eyes are yellow around the brow,
Z is for the sound you make when sleeping which is what
I'm thinking of doing now.

The Magic Staff

Chapter 1

Once there lived a king called Marvollo. He was the king of a mystical Island called 'The Setting Sun' because it was the shape of a setting sun.

Marvollo was very tall and strong. He had a grey beard (yes, like Santa Claus) and a fine silk robe, to match that he wore some wealthy clothes. Above all he wore a pure gold crown with Rubies, Sapphires, and Emeralds but in the middle was a clear diamond. Marvollo lived in a castle constructed by marble and moonstone. The turrets were as tall as skyscrapers and around the colossal castle was a moat full of vile, vicious, infuriated crocodiles waiting for dinner. So having what he wanted, Marvollo was very happy.

Chapter 2

One day, Marvollo was strolling about The Setting Sun when out of a lake jumped a slimy, ugly and gruesome frog holding a smooth, black staff.

"What are you doing here, you ugly frog?"

"Why; don't you remember me, Max the Magician, your friend!"

Chapter 3

"What happened to you, Max?" asked Marvollo curiously.

"It was an evil wizard called Sentorax," explained Max "He was after my magic staff here."

"Then why didn't you make him disappear?" Marvollo asked again.

"Because he took me by surprise," Max answered. "So now you must get rid of Sentorax!" said Max in a croak.

"But how am I supposed to get rid of someone who can turn people into frogs?" asked Marvollo.

"Ah,but you're going to have magic, aren't you?"

"Well, yeah," admitted Marvollo.

"So are you available to accomplish it?" asked Max.

"Yes" said Marvollo confidently.

Max handed him the staff and at the split second that Marvollo touched it he felt a wonderful tingling sensation spreading from his hand that held the staff. Everything he wore started to revolutionize, his fine silk robe turned into a dark blue cloak covered in moons and stars, his wealthy clothes turned into a black t-shirt and his royal crown was replaced by a pointy wizard's hat (also covered in moons and stars). Max gave Marvollo a magic map which showed where Sentorax was at different times.

"Farewell, good friend and be careful," Max said.

"But how am I going to get there?" asked Marvollo.

"Simple, by magic!" replied Max.

"But I haven't got any magic," said Marvollo.

"Yes you have, you just have to channel it to your brain and use it!" explained Max.

"Yes, I can feel it," said Marvollo, he lifted his staff into the air and roared "I SUMMON THE ELEMENT OF WIND!" and just as if nature had heard his command a gust of wind took him on an adventure that he could never forget.

Chapter 4

Marvollo was soaring like a bird. He couldn't believe that he was on a dangerous quest which could result in his death, however, he was very confident. Suddenly, he was caught up in something, something hazardous.

Chapter 5

Marvollo was trapped in a very tight net which was in a giant cave which belonged to a giant!

Marvollo couldn't reach his staff so he couldn't magic his way out but he looked around and had an idea. He reached out for a big, long piece of slate and on top of it was a smaller rock. Marvollo hit the slate which sent the rock flying through the air towards the roof, it bounced off and knocked off a stalactite which cut the net and freed Marvollo. He grabbed the staff and dashed out of the gloomy cave and out into the sunlight.

Suddenly, he spotted a black cloak whip out of sight, Marvollo looked at the map and sure enough Sentorax was right ahead of him. Marvollo, who was invisible crept up, but using his magical powers Sentorax saw him and sent Marvollo sprawling across the floor and lost his invisibility power and said, "So that's how you want to play, is it?"

"Yes, it is," said Sentorax with a malicious smirk and bellowed, "I CALL ON THE POWER OF SAND!" and sent a cluster of sand which buried Marvollo, but not for long. Marvollo shouted, "I SUMMON THE ELEMENT OF LIGHTNING!" then suddenly a bolt of lightning struck the sand and left a fulgurite that which Marvollo wriggled through. "Now it's time to get rid of you once and for all," Marvollo exclaimed "I CALL ON THE POWER OF THE TECTONIC PLATES AND METEORITES!" and without warning the whole area shook and a crack appeared under Sentorax's feet, next a huge meteorite from the Asteroid belt from between Mars and Jupiter crashed down and the crack got wider and lengthier and as it did so Sentorax got buried, only his head and shoulders showing. Suddenly, Marvollo realized something that what he was doing was wrong. It didn't feel like him. Then he remembered all that his parents had taught him.

"Do you want to be freed?" asked Marvollo,

"Of course I would,"

"Okay, but I'll only free you on one condition..."

"What is it?"

"In this world there are so many poor people, there are also people who have nothing to eat, people with lives corrupted by war. If we work together and establish a world with none of those things the world would be a wonderful place! Are you with me?"

"Yes."

Chapter 6

From then on, Marvollo and Sentorax teamed up to make the world a better place; without war; without hunger and without poverty with their magic and they put up charities and all sorts of things and every single person in the world gave their gratitude to Sentorax and of course, Marvollo!

THE END

The Poem of Similes

As bright as light,
As dark as night,
As fast as seconds,
As easy as reckons,
As rigid as metal,
As dangerous as a kettle,
As violent as a gun,
As scorching as the evening sun,
As cold as an asteroid,
As hazardous as things you should avoid,
As crazy as my teacher,
As wonderful as a feature,
As busy as a bumblebee,
As tired as I am writing this for you to see.

Snakes

Snakes are extraordinary the way they slide
Noiselessly, from side to side,
Agility is what snakes are notorious for,
Killing its prey before it's lifeless on the floor,
Exploratory scientists study more about snakes,
Suppressing them from eating humans as their evening steaks.

WATER

Water is so placid,
But as hazardous as acid,
Waves bursting with powers,
Going on for hours.

Water gives us drink and rain galore,
Covering up the ocean floor,
Water gives fish a place to roam,
Under all of the bubbly foam,
Water also tortures boats and freezes paths,
It is also used to fill up baths,
Water is not hard to seek,
That's what makes Earth unique.

A Thank you Letter to Mr. Willy Wonka

"Bedtime Jimmy!" Mum called from the kitchen, "Come on, off to bed,"

"OK, Mum," Jimmy answered dragging himself and the heavy weight of his sleepiness upstairs.

He changed into his pyjamas and clambered into bed.

****

Suddenly, Jimmy woke up. He just couldn't get to sleep. He looked at the clock. It was exactly midnight. The 'Witching Hour' as Roald Dahl liked to call it. Yes, Jimmy loved books, especially Roald Dahl's ones. He thought they were funny, comical, enthralling and also masterpieces. In fact, he decided on reading one now. He crept out of bed, tiptoed to his gargantuan bookshelf (which he had alphabetically ordered) and slipped out a book: Charlie and the Chocolate Factory. He took it to his bed and switched a table lamp on. It flickered once and then shone with an immense light to rival the Sun. As soon as the pure light flooded onto the paper of the book, Jimmy read. The hours crept by; his eyelids feeling heavy and his head drooping on to his feathery pillow...

****

The first thing that Jimmy saw in the morning when he woke up was two pieces of the finest A4 paper: his paper! And a glossy, gleaming, glistening pen: his pen! His favourite pen! In addition to all of that there was neat, immaculate handwriting on that piece of paper: his handwriting! Jimmy tried to remember writing that letter but all he could remember was a dream...

No.1 Bucket and Spade St,
Chocolate Town,
SF99 OBS, UK
13th October 2014

No.1 Choc Block,
Chocolate Town,
SF99 OCB, UK

Dear Mr Wonka,

Having had such a splendiferous time at your esteemed Chocolate Factory, I wanted to thank you for your time. I enjoyed myself very much and Grandpa was thoroughly excited. He was still going on about those marvellous concoctions of yours. I myself was completely astounded (in a brilliant way) of the Chocolate Room.

When I found out that I had the final Golden Ticket, I felt as though I could reach the universe with my fingers, yes, I was that proud. Outside the colossal, towering gates I could literally taste the airy chocolate with the tip of my tongue. Before very long, the gates opened and we went inside the intricate building accompanied by the one and only Mr Willy Wonka himself.

Despite the fact that we lost the other children on the tour, it was thrilling to go around all of the rooms observing the terrific inventions of yours.

My most favourite room was the renowned Chocolate Room where everything was edible. Even a few blades of grass would satisfy you like you had wolfed down a complete cooked dinner, and don't get me started on the Chocolate River: its taste is so mouth-wateringly lush it would transport you into a whole different universe; a chocolate universe.

After that, we went to the Inventing Room where anything and everything is possible. You had made a stick of chewing gum which had the flavour of a three-course meal and without permission, Violet Beauregard took and ate it, what a silly and ignorant little girl.

Mr Wonka, I have just had the most brillioso idea for a new chocolate bar; The Whipple Scrumptious Golden Ticket Delight. Another is the Wonka's Star Bar; a rather nutty chocolate bar sprinkled with star dust. If I can make another suggestion, may I suggest doing the tour again, but, instead of going on foot to rooms, why not use the extraordinary Great Glass Elevator.

Overall, I want to thank you for that terrific day in your remarkable Chocolate Factory, and for letting me view some of the rooms. I hope to see you again.

Yours Sincerely,

Jimmy

FIREWORKS

My dad lets go of the rocket,
It whistles up high,
It looks mesmerizing,
Radiating the sky,

The firework continues,
It tears through the clouds,
It rumbles like thunder,
Almighty and proud,

I wait in anticipation,
For the firework to explode,
It does and falls down in embers,
A story being told!

We light up fireworks,
On Bonfire Night,
We do this to remember,
The 5th of November.

Animals

Animals with fur,
Animals that purr,
Animals with wings,
Animals that sing,
Animals who hiss,
Animals in bliss,
Bats who shriek,
Eagles that seek,
Frogs that croak,
Monkeys who joke,
Busy bees,
Cheeky chimpanzees,
Sneaky rat,
Quiet cat,
A crocodile that's feisty,
What we should do is to treat them nicely!

The Mouse Who Travelled Through Time

There was once a mouse who was a super – genius in everything; you could ask him anything you like and without a shadow of a doubt he would answer correctly. He had had all A-stars in his mouse exams, completed the London Matriculation and had even won the Mouse of the Year trophy (made of cheese) for his brilliance. So you see, he really was a gifted mouse. Although he was really intelligent, he was timid and modest and had bright twinkling blue eyes, sleek dazzling white fur that was well – groomed and also a coiled tail as long as an endless rope.

The mouse lived with his cousin, Rat, in a hole in a lab belonging to a scientist where he had everything he required for his experiments as an inventor. He would spend all his time brooding over different inventions – his latest was a Time Machine.

One night he had a brainwave. He was devouring a meal of the finest cheese with Rat when all of a sudden his expression went wild with exhilaration as he seized a blackboard and chalk stick, then began to skim over the board leaving an elaborate sketch of a Time Machine, an unimaginably perfect Time machine but it was surprisingly fuelled by mouldy cheese.

It took the mouse several weeks to build the parts and assemble the Time Machine. At last, it was ready for lift-off. The mouse set the controls for the beginning of the universe, flicked a switch and WHOOSH!!!

He was off; travelling through time.

All the mouse could see was the inside of a monstrous spiralling Time Vortex...

Suddenly, the mouse heard a great sucking noise and was blasted out into the silent vacuums of Space "Hang on a sec, this isn't the beginning of the universe, of course, I've ran out of cheese." The mouse realized. He looked around and in the distance he spotted the bold letters of Gemini 12: the spacecraft from which Buzz Aldrin did his spacewalk. The mouse steered the Time machine towards Gemini 12 and as he did so he spotted a figure attached by a tether to Gemini 12: Buzz Aldrin! "Wait a minute, if Buzz Aldrin is doing his spacewalk now, this must be 1966; I've travelled a century into the past. The mouse reached Buzz Aldrin, clambered out and stammered "It is an honour to meet you, Sir," (Luckily, the mouse is so clever he knows English) "Who are you and what are you doing so far away from home?" asked Buzz.

"I'm the mouse and I have made a Time Machine and travelled from 2066 to this time zone,"

"You're from the future? Then you must be a very clever mouse, how would you like to do a spacewalk with me?"

Then the mouse became the first of his kind to do a spacewalk. They wandered about for a while and then suddenly they witnessed the biggest type of explosion in space: a Hypernova! Luckily, they were out of the blast radius. They gazed at the spectacular light display and the next moment, the mouse found a particularly mouldy piece of cheese floating out towards him; he grabbed it and had an idea. He opened the engines of the Time Machine and placed the cheese into it. "Well," he said "That's my cue. Farewell, Dr. Aldrin, until next time." The mouse then did some kind of salute with his tail and clambered into the Time Machine, went back into his own time zone and wrote a book about all of his adventures and that's what you just finished reading now!

THE END

I went to the Zoo

I went to the zoo,
Having wanted the loo,
My mother brought me to the lavatories,
But all we found was a hive of bees,
Infuriated, they chased us into a room,
This contained a peculiar broom,
Next we saw a tarantula appear,
Which, automatically filled us with fear,
We ran inside the Reptile House,
We tried not to rouse,
Suddenly the fluorescent light flickers,
My mum whips a torch from her knickers,
From the torch light a snake turned its head around,
It looked at a door, hence, the toilet was found.

A Week of Funny Weather

Monday's gales swept the land,
Forcing insects into sand,
Tuesday's rain pittered and pattered,
School was cancelled, like that mattered,
Wednesday's snow floated like leaves on water,
Unfortunately, our car couldn't start its motor,
Thursday's frost covered the grass,
From afar it looked really class,
Friday's ice made my hands sore,
The ice was so hard it wouldn't thaw,
Saturday's thunder storm raged furiously,
And all my brother did was peer curiously,
Sunday's hot sun came at last,
But alas it left very fast!

That Flowing River

The river riots against the rocks
It streams so fast it blows your socks
The river rages as the wind strikes hard
Water shatters resembling glass shards.

The water gushes down waterfalls
Where pebbles lie as round as balls
Water whines as it smashes against rock
It runs swift all around the clock.

The river is home to millions of creatures
Each one with different features
The river races almighty and robust
The wind flipping the water with a simple thrust.

At last the river calms, flowing in slow strides
Collecting with it magnificent tides
The proud river gushes gracefully
As it comes to rest in the continual sea.

The Plants, the Professor and the Mystery

Chapter 1

It was another sunny, humid, blazing day in SunnyVille and everyone was as cheerful as usual. People were sunbathing in their front gardens trying to get a tan, riding their bikes as fast as the wind and playing football in the streets. The neatly terraced houses shone in their full glory flooded in the beam of the sun, and in one of these houses lived John Zipper!

John Zipper was a skinny boy of eleven with mud – brown hair which was very untidy and acid green eyes, he wore skinny jeans and a green jacket to match his eyes. John had a mad craze for Science and a taste for mysteries. He was well-mannered, confident and also intelligent. His hobby was gardening, he especially liked it if it was with his dad. He was carrying out an experiment on chemicals when suddenly a voice boomed from downstairs "Come down John, we're going to the allotment." It was his dad. John's dad owned a huge allotment and it was his business. He would grow plants and sell them in the market. John stepped in and out of the chemicals and reached the door, he went down the steps and saw his dad, and he had dark green wellingtons and blue overalls. He also had a sun hat over his mousey-brown hair tinged with grey. "Are you ready to go, John," said dad "We'll only be planting seeds today." John put his wellingtons on and walked happily towards the allotment but what he didn't know is that there was a horrendous surprise waiting for him!

The walk to the allotment was long but at last they came to the rusty, ancient, iron gate and amid the loud squelches of the mud they could hear birds chirping as if it were their birthdays. They walked around the shed and a horrifying sight hit their eyes: the plants were dead! Dad was petrified but that didn't stop him from investigating the crime scene (if you could call it one) and looking for clues. John imitated him and looked under the soil and leaves. "I wonder how this happened?" asked John to himself. "Hey, John, come over here, I found something!" shouted Dad. He was at the vegetable patch. "Coming," replied John, he walked over and gasped – the vegetables were as good as new. "What on Earth-" he exclaimed.

"I know, it looks like someone's just come down and done something to the inedible plants and just scampered off," explained Dad "But nobody has the key to the allotment except us," said John "So there's no way someone could've slipped into the allotment,"

"Well... I don't know about you, but I'm getting hungry 'cos of all this thinking and I need some food – it's getting dark anyway," said Dad "We have to get home quickly, otherwise... well you know what mum's like."

"Ok," said John, "I'll close the gate." The pair of them walked back to the gate and as John closed the rusty gate, he spotted a piece of red and blue cloth and had just managed a glance at it before his dad's voice rang out in the gloomy silence of the night, “Coming, Dad,” shouted John as he pocketed the cloth and sprinted off into the darkness.

Chapter 2

“So what are you gonna do?” asked Fred, he was a short boy with a fringe that was blond and he wore baggy jeans and a V-neck jumper. Fred was kind and generous and also had the love for mysteries. He was very confident – except for one thing, he was claustrophobic (scared of small and crammed spaces) and he was John’s best friend.

“Well, I was planning on going down to the allotment and investigating ,” said John, having called Fred down his house and explained to him what had happened at the allotment. “Hey, John, can I have another look at that cloth?” asked Fred,

“Yeah, sure, go on,” said John, handing Fred the piece of cloth. Fred took it and gazed at it turning it around in his hands for about three minutes and suddenly spoke “It looks as if it has been ripped off vigorously,” said Fred.

“I know, and we won’t know any more if we just sit here and talk about it! I’ve got a gut feeling that there is more to this mystery than what meets the eye,” said John getting up and walking out of the door “Well, come on then!”

Both of them walked down to the allotment and at long last they approached the ancient gate that was as rusty as the surface of Mars. They searched for about an hour and then suddenly Fred cried out, “Quick, I found something – hurry!”

"Ok, I'm coming," replied John running over. Fred was bent over something but as John came closer he could see that he was bent over a leaf on the soil. John knelt down, "What is it?" he asked.

"Look," said Fred, pointing to a drop of liquid on the leaf,

"It looks like a chemical but one that I've never seen before," said John opening one of those re-sealable bags and carefully tilting the leaf so that the drop fell into the bag. "Well there's no point in searching now... it's too late, I have to get home for tea – we're having fish 'n' chips!" said John,

"Hey! Do you think there's enough time for us to pop down to the Candy Cove?" asked Fred eagerly,

"Of course!" replied John his face lightening up with enthusiasm "Let's go right now!"

"I've got £10 in my pocket," said Fred,

"Perfect – I've got £5.50, that'll be more than enough for two extra-large packets of liquorice allsorts!" as they headed for The Candy Cove. The Candy Cove was a confectionary shop and John and Fred thought and knew that it was the best shop in the world. Nearly every shelf was packed with jars of peppermint, lollipops, dolly-mixtures, jelly beans, hum-bugs, Haribo's, fruit chews, chocolate bars, after-eight mints and so many more but, the boys' favourite sweet were the Giant Gobstoppers, they were simply enormous and you could suck it for years and years and years and years and you wouldn't see a difference, but that isn't the reason the boys liked it so, it was because of the luscious flavours it concealed – blueberry, raspberry, liquorice, mint, chocolate, vanilla, toffee and caramel. But the only, unfortunate thing was that it cost £60!

The boys entered the shop and a blast of warm, sugary air hit them. Mr Cameron, the shopkeeper was a stout man with a plump, kind face. The boys picked out the liquorice allsorts, brought them to the till and put the money on the counter. Mr Cameron smiled at them and said "The usual, boys?"

"Yes, Mr Cameron," replied John with a warm smile,

"Oh, I remember the time when I was a kid. I used to love liquorice allsorts…" Mr Cameron drifted into a monologue and suddenly, John spotted something on a newspaper "What's this?" whispered John. "Look," Fred looked up and grabbed the newspaper and thought, there was 50p change – just enough for a newspaper!

"Um… Mr Cameron,"

"Yes, m'boy," said Mr Cameron returning to earth,

"Could I have this newspaper, please?"

"Sure you can, m'boy,"

"Thanks," Fred said as he and John left the shop.

"Would you just look at this," said John walking home and he held up the newspaper for Fred to see and summarized what the newspaper said: "A top-secret chemical which was kept by the government has been stolen on the sixth of July-"

"Hey, wasn't that the day before your plants died!" interrupted Fred, "Yes and that's why it's so important, it happened the day before the plants died, it could have been this chemical that killed the plants!" explained John "It's getting late anyway, we should hurry," and with that they sped home.

John typed in his password and logged in, his face illuminated by the glare of the computer. He was doing some research on the chemical. He googled it and not many results came up, however, he chose the top one; suddenly a picture of a young man wearing a lab coat and holding a glass vial containing a clear liquid filled a corner of the screen and small writing filled the rest. John read it and all of a sudden the clues came together like that of a jigsaw piece. John went to sleep knowing that the mystery was as good as solved!

Chapter 3

John met up with Fred the next day. "I've got his address," said John showing him a piece of paper. "Cool," said Fred. "I'll put the address onto my GPS," he typed the address in to his phone and a map appeared on the screen. Last night, John had found the address of the main suspect. Fred and John walked round the corner and came to a dark alleyway. "I've never come here before," said Fred.

"Me neither," said John brushing away cobwebs from his hair. "Come on." They walked on and finally met their destination: the cobwebbed streets of Shadow Lane. They searched for the right door and knocked. There was a few seconds of silence and then the thud of footsteps was heard and the door slowly opened revealing a person with wispy grey hair and a wrinkled face. "Well, well, well, what do we have here, eh?" he rasped.

"Professor McGillerton," John thought.

“We know your secret, McGillerton,” he said in a bold voice and McGillerton turned around quick enough to see Fred in his house, tipping a clear liquid into a resealable bag and running towards where John was right then, McGillerton lunged at Fred, but he ducked whilst McGillerton sprawled into one of the walls. “We know everything and all we needed was the evidence and now we’ll just be off to the police and find you a nice, cosy prison cell and-”

“- Oh, no you don’t!” McGillerton interrupted and grabbed the boys by the shoulder and held them up, “You’re not going anyway until I deal with you!” and he brought them into the house. It was dim and shadows loomed everywhere, it was a strange and dismal place. McGillerton threw them into a corner of what seemed like a living room and tied their hands and feet with a fisherman’s knot and as he did so Fred spotted McGillerton’s socks, they were red and blue – the exact pattern as the piece of cloth and what’s more was that there was a big hole in them. “Look, it’s the same pattern,” said Fred,

“Yes it is, he must be the culprit.” McGillerton brought out a cage from inside a cupboard. In the cage was what looked like a clump of brownish-green seaweed. "Come out, you useless animal!" shouted McGillerton and suddenly the thing writhed and slithered into the form of a Boa Constrictor, but it didn't come out to the boys' pleasure. "Maybe you'll come out by the temptation of some nice food." McGillerton croaked as he went to the kitchen leaving the boys and the snake. "Hey! You've got your phone, haven't you?" asked John,

"Yeah, why?" answered Fred,

"Isn't it obvious, we call the police."

"Yes, I know, but how?" said Fred "I can't reach my phone,"

"Mmmm........... hang on! I collected a few rocks for my rock collection – there's bound to be some jagged stones. Think you can reach 'em?"

"Oh .... I get it," said Fred turning his body round so that his hands were aligned with John's pockets. He took a stone and managed to rub it against the ropes holding John in position. After the boys were released, Fred called the police. Luckily, Fred's dad was a policeman and he was there in an instant. They hand-cuffed McGillerton and gave the snake to the Pet Control centre. The police asked John to explain and that he did. "It all started with the Best Scientist contest. Professor McGillerton made a toxin that if it entered the human body it will enhance the brain. McGillerton thought it was a stroke of genius but the judges thought differently, they said it was dangerous as it contained a hazardous chemical that could kill that human so they confiscated it and McGillerton was furious, he had spent all his life on that and it was over. After that, he turned to a life of crime, stealing things and selling them just to earn a living but then he was caught in the act of stealing, not by the police but by an ordinary person. This person was kind, trying to change the evil, twisted ways of McGillerton and he was successful for a short time. The person had persuaded McGillerton to become an acrobat and to stop his evil ways but after McGillerton had gained his trust, he offered to take him to Australia pretending to repay him for his good deeds but McGillerton was actually planning on leaving him behind. But why? Because of something that the person had let slip – they were talking of the Best Scientist contest when the person said that he knew a person who knew one of the judges. McGillerton weaselled the details out of him and McGillerton weaved a diabolical scheme to finally win the contest. With that person out of the way, McGillerton reverted back to his evil ways, but for his plan to work, he had to steal the confiscated toxin and alter it so that once it enters the body McGillerton could control that body by his own thoughts. When he had concocted the toxin properly, he needed to find a way to give it to the judge, but how? By using that person's information of course-"

"But who was that person who knew the judge?" interrupted Fred's dad,

"It was my dad," replied John,

"What!" everybody cried in unison "Your dad?"

"Yes," said John "That judge is a regular customer of my dad. McGillerton, using his acrobatic skills climbed the wall to the allotment but one of his socks got caught on the gate. He dropped the toxin into the soil and scampered off. He hoped that the judge would eat the vegetables which had soaked in the toxin."

"But then why didn't the toxin work?" asked Fred's dad.

"Because the immense heat weakened the toxin." replied John. "Well, we'd better give you a reward as you saved the police a heap of trouble," said Fred's dad standing up, "Is there anything in particular you like?"

"Hmm...... there is one thing..." said John and Fred.

And that's how John Zipper ended up with the world's biggest gobstopper!

THE END